PRESENTED TO:

....

FROM:

....

You Are
Special

A Story for Everyone

ILLUSTRATIONS BY SERGIO MARTINEZ

Max Lucado

CANDLE
BOOKS

You Are Special
Text copyright ©1993, 1997, 2002 by Max Lucado
Illustrations copyright ©1997, 2002 by Sergio Martinez
Published in the USA by Crossway Books *a division of Good News Publishers.*

The right of Max Lucado to be identified as the author of this work and Sergio
Martinez to be identified as the illustrator of this work has been asserted by them in
accordance with the Copyright, Designs and Patents Act 1988.

Published by Candle Books
an imprint of
Lion Hudson plc
Wilkinson House, Jordan Hill Road,
Oxford OX2 8DR, England
www.lionhudson.com/candle

ISBN 978 1 85985 590 4

First edition 2005

The publisher wishes to acknowledge that the text for *You Are Special*
appeared originally in *Tell Me the Secrets,* written by Max Lucado and
illustrated by Ron DiCianni.

A catalogue record for this book is available from the British Library

Printed and bound in Malaysia, October 2014, LH18

Other titles in this series:
You Are Mine

THE
WEMMICKS

THE WEMMICKS were small wooden people carved by a woodworker named Eli. His workshop sat on a hill overlooking their village.

Each Wemmick was different. Some had big noses, others had large eyes. Some were tall and others were short. Some wore hats, others wore coats. But all were made by the same carver, and all lived in the village.

And all day, every day, the Wemmicks did the same thing: They gave each other stickers. Each Wemmick had a box of golden star stickers and a box of grey dot stickers. Up and down the streets all over the city, people spent their days sticking stars or dots on one another.

The pretty ones, those with smooth wood and fine paint, always got stars. But if the wood was rough or the paint chipped, the Wemmicks gave dots.

The talented ones got stars, too. Some could lift big sticks high above their heads or jump over tall boxes. Still others knew big words or could sing pretty songs. Everyone gave them stars.

Some Wemmicks had stars all over them! Every time they got a star, it made them feel so good! It made them want to do something else and get another star.

Others, though, could do little. They got dots.

Punchinello was one of these. He tried to jump high like the others, but he always fell. And when he fell, the others would gather around and give him dots.

Sometimes when he fell, his wood got scratched, so the people would give him more dots.

Then when he would try to explain why he had fallen, he would say something silly, and the Wemmicks would give him more dots.

After a while he had so many dots that he didn't want to go outside. He was afraid he would do something silly such as forget his hat or step in the water, and then people would give him another dot. In fact, he had so many grey dots that some people came up and gave him dots for no reason at all.

"He deserves lots of dots," the wooden people would agree with one another.

"He's not a good wooden person."

After a while Punchinello believed them. "I'm not a good Wemmick," he would say.

The few times he went outside, he hung around other Wemmicks who also had a lot of dots. He felt better around them.

LUCIA

ONE DAY Punchinello met a
Wemmick who was unlike any he'd ever
met. She had no dots or stars. She was
just wooden. Her name was Lucia.

It wasn't that people didn't try to give
her stickers; it was just that the stickers
didn't stick. Some of the Wemmicks
admired Lucia for having no dots, so they
would run up and give her a star. But it
would fall off.

Others looked down on her for having no stars, so they would give her a dot. But that wouldn't stick either.

That's the way I want to be, thought Punchinello.

I don't want anyone's marks.

So he asked the stickerless Wemmick how she did it.

"It's easy," Lucia replied. "Every day I go to see Eli."

"Eli?"

"Yes, Eli. The woodcarver. I sit in the workshop with him."

"Why?"

"Why don't you find out for yourself? Go up the hill. He's there." And with that the Wemmick who had no stickers turned and skipped away.

"But will he want to see me?" Punchinello cried out. Lucia didn't hear.

So Punchinello went home. He sat near a window and watched the wooden people as they scurried around giving each other stars and dots.

"It's not right," he muttered to himself. And he decided to go and see Eli.

THE
WOODCARVER

PUNCHINELLO walked up the narrow
path to the top of the hill and stepped
into the big shop. His wooden eyes
widened at the size of everything. The
stool was as tall as he was. He had to
stretch on his tiptoes to see the top of the
workbench. A hammer was as long as his
arm. Punchinello swallowed hard. "I'm
not staying here!" And he turned to leave.

Then he heard his name.

"Punchinello?" The voice was deep and strong.

Punchinello stopped.

"Punchinello! How good to see you. Come and let me have a look at you."

Punchinello turned slowly and looked at the large bearded craftsman. "You know my name?" the little Wemmick asked.

"Of course I do. I made you."

Eli stooped down and picked him up and set him on the bench. "Hmm," the maker spoke thoughtfully as he looked at the grey dots. "Looks like you've been given some bad marks."

"I didn't mean to, Eli. I really tried hard."

"Oh, you don't have to defend yourself to me, child."

"I don't care what the other Wemmicks think."

"You don't?"

"No, and you shouldn't either. Who are they to give stars or dots? They're Wemmicks just like you. What they think doesn't matter, Punchinello. All that matters is what I think. And I think you are very special."

Punchinello laughed. "Me, special? Why? I can't walk fast. I can't jump. My paint is peeling. Why do I matter to you?"

Eli looked at Punchinello, put his hands on those small wooden shoulders, and spoke very slowly. "Because you're mine. That's why you matter to me."

Punchinello had never had anyone look at him like this — much less his maker. He didn't know what to say.

"Every day I've been hoping you'd come," Eli explained.

"I came because I met someone who had no marks," said Punchinello.

"I know. She told me about you."

"Why don't the stickers stay on her?"

The maker spoke softly. "Because she has decided that what I think is more important than what they think. The stickers only stick if you let them."

"What?"

"The stickers only stick if they matter to you. The more you trust my love, the less you care about their stickers."

"I'm not sure I understand."

Eli smiled. "You will, but it will take time. You've got a lot of marks. For now, just come to see me every day and let me remind you how much I care."

Eli lifted Punchinello off the bench and set him on the ground.

"Remember," Eli said as the Wemmick walked out of the door, "you are special because I made you. And I don't make mistakes."

Punchinello didn't stop, but in his heart he thought, *I think he really means it.*

And when he did, a dot fell to the ground.